Haunted

Phantom Flames

Spellbound

An Imprint of Magic Wagon
abdopublishing.com

By Rich Wallace Illustrated By Daniela Volpari

abdopublishing.com

Published by Magic Wagon, a division of ABDO, PO Box 398166,
Minneapolis, Minnesota 55439. Copyright © 2017 by Abdo
Consulting Group, Inc. International copyrights reserved in all
countries. No part of this book may be reproduced in any form
without written permission from the publisher. Spellbound™ is a
trademark and logo of Magic Wagon.

Printed in the United States of America, North Mankato, Minnesota.
052016
092016

Written by Rich Wallace
Illustrated by Daniela Volpari
Edited by Heidi M.D. Elston
Designed by Laura Mitchell

Library of Congress Cataloging-in-Publication Data

Names: Wallace, Rich, author. | Volpari, Daniela, 1985- illustrator.
Title: Phantom flames / by Rich Wallace ; illustrated by Daniela Volpari.
Description: Minneapolis, MN : Magic Wagon, 2017. | Series: Haunted
Identifiers: LCCN 2015048143 | ISBN 9781624021503 (print) | ISBN
9781680779653 (ebook)
Subjects: LCSH: Stu and his friend Dan are hiking in the forest when a
   rainstorm leads them to seek shelter in a haunted hunting cabin, which
   suddenly bursts into flames in the middle of the night--the boys escape
   with their lives, but when Stu returns in the day he finds the cabin
   apparently untouched by fire, but in the possession of a ghost that
   clearly does not want company. | Ghost stories. | Haunted houses--Juvenile
   fiction. | Fire--Juvenile fiction. | CYAC: Ghosts--Fiction. | Haunted
   houses--Fiction. | Fire--Fiction.
Classification: LCC PZ7.W15877 Ph 2016 | DDC 813.54--dc23
LC record available at http://lccn.loc.gov/2015048143

Table of Contents

Chapter 1
Get Out!

A storm was on its way. I told
Dan we should head for home.
He *shook* his head and kept hiking.

"This is a campout, not a wimp out,
Stu," Dan said. "We have a good tent.
A little *rain* won't hurt us."

4

I glanced at the sky. **DARK** clouds were coming toward us. Thunder rumbled in the distance.

Dan moved *FASTER* on the trail.
We were hoping for a nice campfire,
but the **rain** started quickly. It
would be hard to start a fire with wet
wood.

The rain turned to a DOWNPOUR. My clothing was soaked, and I was shivering. My new sneakers were caked with mud. "We'll never dry out in this storm," I said.

"There's a hunting cabin up ahead," Dan said. "It's never locked."

"Sounds better than a soggy tent," I replied. But I wasn't so sure.

I'd heard rumors about that cabin. "They say that place is HAUNTED," I mumbled.

"The only haunts in there are mice and spiders," Dan said with a laugh.

The cabin smelled MUSTY inside. It was one small room with two wooden bunks and a fireplace. There was a stack of dry wood, so we were warm in a few minutes.

Dan hung his socks by the fire.
They STUNK! I sat on one of the
bunks and unwrapped a sandwich.
Dan plopped down on the other bunk.

The *wind* rattled the cabin. Rain slashed against the lone window. It was **DARK** as night except for the fire.

The flames cast a glow on the wall. A **SHADOW** in the glow gave me a fright. It looked like two eyes and a snarling mouth.

The mouth seemed to open. *"Get out!"* it hissed.

13

Chapter 2

Run!

"Who said that?" Dan asked, sitting up. I *POINTED* at the wall. The **FACE** had disappeared.

Dan opened the cabin door. "Who's out there?" he **CALLED**. There was no answer.

"It was probably the fire," I said. "Wood *hisses* sometimes when it BURNS. Maybe some of the rain leaked down the chimney."

"Sounded like a voice," Dan said.

I thought so, too. And maybe I'd imagined that **SPOOKY** face, but it sure had me worried.

Dan told some jokes and *ghost* stories. I kept staring at that wall until the fire went out.

Dan was soon *snoozing*, but I was wide awake. It felt as if someone were **watching** me.

Someone

who didn't want

me to be there.

I finally nodded off. After midnight, I felt a **punch** in the ribs. *"Cut it out!"* I yelled.

"Cut what out?" Dan asked.

"Why did you HIT me?"

"I haven't moved," Dan said.

"Well, somebody did it."

A strong smell of SMOKE

made me sneeze. I shined my

flashlight toward the fireplace,

but the FLAMES were out.

SMOKE filled the cabin. Dan coughed. My eyes were stinging.

A sudden FLASH of light nearly blinded me. An entire wall of the cabin BURST into flame. The heat made my face sting like sunburn.

"RUN!" I shouted.

I felt a strong **SHOVE**

backward as I jumped from the bunk.

Something seemed to *grab* my arm.

I YANKED free, and we hurried
away from the cabin. I didn't even put
on my sneakers.

We stood in the *rain* as the cabin **BURNED** to the ground. Barefoot and *freezing*, we stumbled along the trail toward home.

Chapter 3
Push Back

I hated losing my new **sneakers**.
Could they have **survived**
the fire? Dan and I walked back to
the cabin the next morning. I was
SHOCKED to see it still standing.
There was no sign of a fire!

"That can't be," I said. "This must be a **different** cabin."

"There's only one cabin out this way," Dan said. "That's it."

The door was **LOCKED**.

I looked in the window and saw my **sneakers** and knapsack. What happened to the fire? Nothing was **CHARRED**.

I tried the door again. No luck.

"That door is never LOCKED," Dan

said. "I don't think it even has a lock."

I pulled harder. Then I felt a

SHOVE, and I fell back.

"What happened?" Dan asked.

"SOMETHING pushed me," I said.
I stared at the door and SHOOK
my head. "I'm not leaving without
my stuff."

"Try the window, Stu," Dan said.

It opened easily, and I **BOOSTED** myself up. But the window came *CRASHING* down on my head. That **HURT**.

"Hold it up for me," I said.

Dan lifted the window and braced his hands against it. The window **SMACKED** my head again.

"Can't you hold that?" I said, rubbing my forehead.

"It weighs a ton," Dan said.

"It does not," I replied.

"Well, then SOMETHING was pushing back," Dan said. "Let's get out of here. This is *freaking* me out."

Dan ran off. I tried to lift the window again. A FLAME rose from the sill.

This was creepy. I knew I could be in and out of that cabin in a second if I could just get inside.

I RAN to catch up to Dan. But I'd be back. I'd return with a hammer and BUST down that door.

Chapter 4

Stay Away

I headed back to the cabin that evening. **Alone**. I'd spent a lot on those **sneakers**.

I wasn't **leaving** without them

The door opened easily this time. Dan was right. There was no lock. It must have been JAMMED before. Or maybe something *evil* was forcing it closed.

It was freezing cold in the cabin. Much colder than outside. My breath came out in a misty cloud. I shivered hard.

I picked up my **flashlight** and shined it around the room. Everything was the way we'd left it. No sign of a FIRE.

I changed into my new sneakers and **STUFFED** the old ones into my knapsack. Suddenly the *chill* was gone. The room felt like a **BLASTING** furnace.

A sizzling sound made me turn. The door was on fire! FLAMES leaped up the wall, and the room filled with SMOKE.

The window was my only chance to **ESCAPE**. But I couldn't get it open. I choked on the **SMOKE** and **DROPPED** to the floor. My sleeve caught fire, and I banged it against my leg to put it out.

I had to **SMASH** the window. Where was my hammer? I couldn't see anything through the **SMOKE**, so I reached blindly around the floor. The heat was UNBEARABLE.

Suddenly the window flew open. I *scrambled* toward it, and felt myself being lifted from behind. My hands BURNED as I gripped the sill and climbed out.

The window SLAMMED behind me. A face in the glass yelled, "Stay away from here!"

He wouldn't have to tell me twice.

I stumbled away from the cabin and watched as the flames died out. Within minutes, the cabin looked the same as before. No DAMAGE. No sign of a fire at all. The old ghost had saved my life. But his message was clear: "Leave me and my cabin alone!"